Rain

A Level One Reader

By Alice K. Flanagan

The Child's World®

Drip, drip. Splash!
Here comes the rain!

Rain comes from clouds. But how does rain become rain?

The sun heats water in puddles, lakes, rivers, and oceans.

As water heats up, it turns into a gas. This gas rises into the air.

As the gas cools, it turns into tiny drops of water. They form clouds.

The drops become too heavy for the cloud. Then they fall as rain.

Too much rain can
cause flooding.

Rain flows into the soil, rivers, and oceans.

Then the sun heats the water. The cycle begins again.

All life needs rain.

Word List

cycle

flooding

gas

puddles

splash

Note to Parents and Educators

Welcome to Wonder Books®! These books provide text at three different levels for beginning readers to practice and strengthen their reading skills. Additionally, the use of nonfiction text provides readers the valuable opportunity to *read to learn*, not just to learn to read.

These leveled readers allow children to choose books at their level of reading confidence and performance. Nonfiction Level One books offer beginning readers simple language, word choice, and sentence structure as well as a word list. Nonfiction Level Two books feature slightly more difficult vocabulary, longer sentences, and longer total text. In the back of each Nonfiction Level Two book are an index and a list of books and Web sites for finding out more information. Nonfiction Level Three books continue to extend word choice and length of text. In the back of each Nonfiction Level Three book are a glossary, an index, and a list of books and Web sites for further research.

State and national standards in reading and language arts emphasize using nonfiction at all levels of reading development. Wonder Books® fill the historical void in nonfiction material for the primary grade readers with the additional benefit of a leveled text.

About the Author

Alice K. Flanagan taught elementary school for ten years. Now she writes for children and teachers. She has been writing for more than twenty years. Some of her books include biographies, phonics books, holiday books, and information books about careers, animals, and weather. Alice K. Flanagan lives with her husband in Chicago, Illinois.

Published by The Child's World®
P.O. Box 326
Chanhassen, MN 55317-0326
800-599-READ
www.childsworld.com

Photo Credits
© Adam Jones/The Image Bank: 9
© Craig Tuttle/CORBIS: 5, 17, 21
© Ed Bock/CORBIS: cover
© Grafton M. Smith/CORBIS: 18
© Jurgen Vogt/The Image Bank: 13
© Lester Lefkowitz/CORBIS: 6
© Michael S. Lewis/CORBIS: 10
© Reuters NewMedia Inc./CORBIS: 14
© Richard Price/Taxi: 2

Editorial Directions, Inc.: E. Russell Primm and Emily J. Dolbear, Editors;
Alice K. Flanagan, Photo Research; Emily J. Dolbear, Photo Selector

The Child's World®: Mary Berendes, Publishing Director

Library of Congress Cataloging-in-Publication Data
Flanagan, Alice K.
Rain / by Alice K. Flanagan.
    p. cm. — (Wonder books)
Summary: Simple text describes rain, its characteristics, how it is
formed, and its effects on the Earth.
Includes bibliographical references and index.
  ISBN 1-56766-452-0 (lib. bdg. : alk. paper)
1. Rain and rainfall—Juvenile literature. [1. Rain and rainfall.]
I. Title. II. Series: Wonder books (Chanhassen, Minn.)
  QC924.7 .F55 2003
  551.57'7—dc21
                    2002151611